The Story of Jesus' Birth
Matthew 1:18–24 and Luke 2:1–20 for children

Written by Nicole E. Dreyer
Illustrated by Len Ebert

Arch® Books
Copyright © 2002 Concordia Publishing House
3558 S. Jefferson Avenue, St. Louis, MO 63118-3968
Manufactured in Colombia

Joseph was a carpenter
Who made things out of wood,
In a shop in Nazareth
Where business was quite good.

Joseph was to marry soon
A woman that he loved.
Mary was his dear one's name;
Both blessed by God above.

One day Joseph heard some news
That took him by surprise.
Mary was to have a child!
An angel had told her why:

"Your child," the angel Gabriel said,
"Will be the Son of God.
And you shall call Him Jesus."
But Joseph said, "That's odd."

So God then sent a special dream
To Joseph in the night.
"Do not fear," an angel said.
"Dear Joseph, it's all right."

Kind Joseph heard God's message.
That dream had changed his life.
So Joseph went to Mary
And took her for his wife.

Caesar was in charge back then.
He sent out this decree:
Everyone now owes a tax.
Go home to pay this fee.

So Joseph went to Bethlehem,
With Mary by his side.
Upon a soft brown donkey,
His pregnant wife did ride.

But when they came to David's town,
As Bethlehem was called,
All the rooms were filled up tight—
Except a manger stall.

Joseph went into that stall
And fixed a bed of hay.
Mary gratefully stretched out
To rest from their long day.

Suddenly the quiet night
Was filled with holy sound.
The animals were wide-awake
And gathered close around.

The birds, and cows, and sheep could see
The babe born in their barn,
As Joseph placed the infant King
Into His mother's arms.

And in the fields not far away,
Some shepherds were surprised
By angels bringing this Good News:
"The Savior has arrived!"

Into the town the shepherds went
To see this newborn one.
And when they came the shepherds said,
"We'd like to see your son."

But Joseph smiled and shook his head,
"This child is *God's* own Son—
Born today to save us all,
This Holy, Precious One."

The shepherds worshiped Jesus,
And we can worship too.
We'll kneel before the Savior
Who loves both me and you!

Dear Parents,

Too often Joseph is a forgotten character in the Christmas story. Think about his situation—the woman he is about to marry is going to have a baby, and he is not the father. Yet he trusts in God and obeys His command. Joseph accepts the responsibility and lovingly cares for Jesus as an earthly father.

The concept of being responsible is difficult to teach. One way to teach this concept is to "flip" the word around, indicating that responsibility is the "ability to respond." And we are blessed with the opportunity to respond to God's love for us in Jesus.

As a family, talk about ways you can be responsible and respond to God's love at the same time. Responsibility often means serving others. Thank God that He sent His Son to serve us as He took the punishment for our sins. Ask Him to help you accept responsibility with a servant heart.

The Editor